GAVIN McNALLY'S YEAR OFF

SAVING THE ALLIGATORS

by Emma Bland Smith
illustrated by Mirelle Ortega

Spellbound
An Imprint of Magic Wagon
abdobooks.com

TO EVERETT -EBS

FOR MY MOM, DAD, AUNT AND BROTHER. -MO

abdobooks.com

Published by Magic Wagon, a division of ABDO, PO Box 398166, Minneapolis, Minnesota 55439. Copyright © 2020 by Abdo Consulting Group, Inc. International copyrights reserved in all countries. No part of this book may be reproduced in any form without written permission from the publisher. Spellbound™ is a trademark and logo of Magic Wagon.

Printed in the United States of America, North Mankato, Minnesota.
052019
092019

Written by Emma Bland Smith
Illustrated by Mirelle Ortega
Edited by Tamara L. Britton
Art Directed by Candice Keimig

Library of Congress Control Number: 2018965019

Publisher's Cataloging-in-Publication Data

Names: Smith, Emma Bland, author. I Ortega, Mirelle, illustrator.
Title: Saving the alligators / by Emma Bland Smith; illustrated by Mirelle Ortega.
Description: Minneapolis, Minnesota : Magic Wagon, 2020. I Series: Gavin McNally's year
   off; book 3
Summary: The McNallys are visiting the Okefenokee National Wildlife Refuge on the
   border of Georgia and Florida. On a swamp tour, Gavin captures two people capturing
   baby alligators on video. He and his father set off in kayaks to investigate. Can they
   notify officials about the poachers and save the alligators?
Identifiers: ISBN 9781532135088 (lib. bdg.) I ISBN 9781532135682 (ebook) I ISBN
   9781532135989 (Read-to-Me ebook)
Subjects: LCSH: Family vacations--Juvenile fiction. I Recreational vehicle living--Juvenile
   fiction. I Poaching--Juvenile fiction. I Rescue work--Juvenile fiction. I American
   alligator--Juvenile fiction.
Classification: DDC [Fic]--dc23

TABLE OF CONTENTS

CHAPTER 1

CAUGHT
ON FILM

"That was so COOL!" said

Chloe, stepping off the tour boat.

Behind her, the Okefenokee swamp

LOOMED still and mysterious.

"Those alligators were CREEPY!"

said Gavin, following her. "I would

not want to swim in there!"

Gus *looked* up from his guidebook. "Alligators hardly ever **ATTACK** humans."

"Hardly ever doesn't mean never," said Gavin.

"Let's go, guys," said Dad, heading for the parking lot. "We have a LONG drive to the campground."

Gavin **slapped** at a mosquito as he climbed into the RV. Here near the Georgia-Florida border, even in March, it was HOT.

Gavin felt a pang of homesickness for his town on the California coast. There, it was probably foggy and cool right now. Crazy to think his family had been on this cross-country road trip for nine months already!

Dad started to drive. Gavin pulled out his camera. He'd taken a lot of COOL pictures and videos during the boat tour.

He SWIPED through photos, then pressed play on a video. Trees, water, an alligator. More trees and water. Wait, what was that red thing in the background? He replayed it. A man was STUFFING something into a bag. But what? Leaves? Trash?

Gavin ZOOMED in.

It was not leaves or trash. It

was a baby alligator!

CHAPTER 2
U-TURN

A chill raced up Gavin's spine. Yep, the man was stuffing a baby alligator into a bag.

Don't JUMP to conclusions, Gavin told himself. The guy probably worked there.

But then **why** wasn't he wearing the uniform?

The guide had mentioned **POACHERS** stealing alligators to sell or use for roadside attractions. Was that *what* this guy was doing?

"I can't believe it," he muttered.

"Can't believe *what*?" asked

Mom, *looking* over her shoulder.

"POACHERS!" said Gavin, passing her the camera. "We have to go back!"

A minute later, Dad was making a U-TURN.

They pulled into the parking lot. Gavin **SPRINTED** toward the dock. The tour boat was out with a **LOAD** of visitors. None of the employees were around. Dad *checked* the office. A sign on the door said, "BACK IN 1 HR."

"The **POACHERS** could be miles away in an hour!" yelled Gavin. "They could be miles away **ALREADY**!"

"I'll call the swamp refuge office," said Mom, *looking* at a brochure. "If I can just get reception." She walked around, holding her phone **UP** in the air.

There wasn't time for that! FRUSTRATED, Gavin walked up to the edge of the dock. Rental kayaks bobbed gently. Life jackets waited for passengers in a pile on the dock. Gavin turned slowly.

"**HEY**, Dad," he *CALLED*.

"Want to go kayaking?"

CHAPTER 3
POACHERS!

Gavin and Dad *glided* out into the swamp.

They **waved** to Mom, Chloe, and Gus. Mom was still trying to get in touch with the authorities. Gavin and Dad's job was to locate the POACHERS and come straight back, without being *seen*.

They rounded a corner. Moss **hung** from the trees, and the filtered sun made it hard to see. Birds squawked; an animal splashed. Already on edge, Gavin JUMPED at every sound.

Another turn. His arms ACHED.
Had they gone too far? Had the
POACHERS already left? Maybe
they should have just waited for
the police, or rangers, or whoever

was in **CHARGE** of this stuff.
Gavin **TURNED** to tell Dad
they should just go back, when—
there, through the trees, was the
man from the video.

"Dad, look!" *hissed* Gavin.

Gavin and Dad paddled closer.

They hid behind a LOW hill.

"**GRAB** that one!" the man was saying. "He'll be our main attraction."

A woman's voice answered, "Okay, but then we have to *LEAVE*."

She was STANDING in the water and holding a metal pole.

Gavin and Dad exchanged an ANXIOUS look. They had to delay the POACHERS until the authorities arrived.

Gavin looked around, DESPERATE for anything that could help. Beyond the POACHERS, he glimpsed a white truck. The getaway vehicle!

CHAPTER 4
IN THE SWAMP

In whispers, Gavin convinced Dad to let him check out the truck. If nothing else, he could get the license plate **NUMBER**. That way the law enforcement people could track down the **POACHERS** later.

"Be careful!" said Dad, as Gavin climbed carefully onto the shore.

He crawled up to the truck. Its windows were open, and unbelievably, the key was in the ignition! Gavin grinned. If he took the key, the POACHERS would be stuck here!

He *TUGGED* out the key. Pausing just to memorize the truck's license plate number, he **CRAWLED** back to the water.

"Now let's hurry!" Gavin whispered. He knew taking the key wouldn't stop the POACHERS forever. The sooner he and Dad could return and report the location, the better!

Frantically, Dad and Gavin tried to find their way back. But in the fading light, everything looked different.

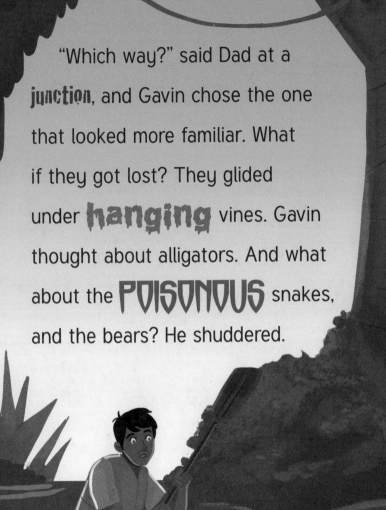

"Which way?" said Dad at a **junction**, and Gavin chose the one that looked more familiar. What if they got lost? They glided under **hanging** vines. Gavin thought about alligators. And what about the **POISONOUS** snakes, and the bears? He shuddered.

"Gavin, *look*!" called Dad. An airboat was **RACING** toward them!

"Over here!" called Gavin, **waving**. They explained everything to the WILDLIFE officers. Gavin told them exactly where to go.

"**GREAT** job," said one of the officers. "Thanks to you, those alligators are going home! Now head *BACK* yourselves. Your family is **worried** about you!"

When they reached the dock,
eager hands **hauled** Gavin up.
Mom **HUGGED** him and
Dad for what felt like minutes.
Chloe took their picture. Gus
wanted to know **EXACTLY** how
many alligators they'd seen.

The tour guide gave Gavin a drink. "It's *sweet* tea, a local specialty," he said. Gavin took a big **gulp**. **Delicious**. He'd never had this in California.

Walking toward the RV, Gavin pictured the baby alligators, more cute than **CREEPY**, really. Smiling, he realized he'd just completed one of his "Personal Projects". *Be a friend to nature.*

A cool breeze blew. Somewhere high above, a bird sang. Suddenly, the swamp seemed like a pretty nice place.